Dear Parent:
Your child's love of reading starts here!

Every child learns to read in a different way and at his or her own speed. Some go back and forth between reading levels and read favorite books again and again. Others read through each level in order. You can help your young reader improve and become more confident by encouraging his or her own interests and abilities. From books your child reads with you to the first books he or she reads alone, there are I Can Read Books for every stage of reading:

SHARED READING
Basic language, word repetition, and whimsical illustrations, ideal for sharing with your emergent reader

BEGINNING READING
Short sentences, familiar words, and simple concepts for children eager to read on their own

READING WITH HELP
Engaging stories, longer sentences, and language play for developing readers

READING ALONE
Complex plots, challenging vocabulary, and high-interest topics for the independent reader

I Can Read Books have introduced children to the joy of reading since 1957. Featuring award-winning authors and illustrators and a fabulous cast of beloved characters, I Can Read Books set the standard for beginning readers.

A lifetime of discovery begins with the magical words "I Can Read!"

Visit www.icanread.com for information
on enriching your child's reading experience.

*For the Black Boys Book Club. Love your
brilliance, imagination, spirit of adventure,
and big hearts. You inspire me.*
—K.S.L.

*For Aria & Sebastian,
your imagination is endless*
—N.M.

I Can Read® and I Can Read Book® are trademarks of HarperCollins Publishers.

Ty's Travels: Beach Day!
Text copyright © 2021 by Kelly Starling Lyons
Illustrations copyright © 2021 by Nina Mata
Library of Congress Control Number: 2020947251
ISBN 978-0-06-295114-4 (trade bdg.)—ISBN 978-0-06-295113-7 (pbk.)

Book design by Rachel Zegar
21 22 23 24 25 LSCC 10 9 8 7 6 5 4 3 2 1

❖
First Edition

My First SHARED READING · **I Can Read!**

TY'S TRAVELS

Beach Day!

by Kelly Starling Lyons   pictures by Nina Mata

HARPER

An Imprint of HarperCollinsPublishers

Ty looks out the window.

The sky is blue.

The sun shines.

What a good day for the beach!

Ty puts on his trunks.

He grabs his pail and toys.

Daddy and Ty go outside.

They step in the warm sand.
Ty wiggles his toes and grins.

Ty and Daddy dig.
They find seashells.
They build a sandcastle.

Ty spots a seagull.

He shows Daddy.

What will Ty see next?

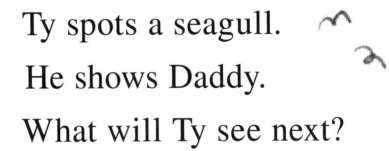

9

Ty wipes his face.
He spots their cooler.

Ty pulls out some ice pops.
They drip and taste so good.
What will Ty see next?

The sea sparkles.

"Come on, Daddy!" Ty says.

Ty runs and splashes.

Daddy splashes, too.

What will Ty see next?

Then Ty hears something.

Thwack.

He looks next door.

All Ty sees is the fence.

Ty spots a beach ball.

Up, up, up.

Then down and thwack.

Up, up, up.

Then down and thwack.

Up, up, up.

Uh-oh.

The ball flies over the fence.

Ty hits the ball back.
Thwack.

Ty spots his friend Jazz.

He's holding the ball.

"Thanks, Ty!" Jazz says, waving.

Ty looks at Daddy.

Daddy smiles and nods.

"Want to come to our beach?"
Ty asks Jazz.
Jazz asks his mom.
He's back in a flash.

Jazz steps in the warm sand.

He wiggles his toes and grins.

Ty and Jazz dig a moat.

They splash!

They surf the waves.

What will they see next?

Ty spots a crab.

What a cool way to move!

Daddy starts them off.

"On your mark, get set, go!"

Ty and Jazz crab race.

What will they see next?

Jazz spots his beach ball.

Thwack!

He hits it to Ty.

Thwack!

Ty hits it to Daddy.

Back and forth.

Again and again.

29

The sun shines.

Ty and Jazz wipe their faces
and plop on the sand.

Ty spots the cooler.

Daddy gets the ice pops.

There's so much to see
at the beach.
Ty saw the best thing of all.
A friend.